This book belongs to

....

The Barefoot Book of

PRINCESSES

retold by Caitlín Matthews
illustrated by Olwyn Whelan

Barefoot Books
Celebrating Art and Story

for Kaitlin Spangler – C.M.

for Megan – O.W.

CONTENTS

The Princess and the Pea

DANISH

Once upon a time, there was a prince who wanted to marry a princess. Not just *any* princess, but a *real* princess. His parents, the kind king and queen, looked far and wide for one. They invited princess after princess to come and visit them.

Some were too thin,
some were too fat,
some did not speak the same language,
some had too many dogs,
some liked horses better than people,
some wore very silly clothes,
some giggled too much,
and some princesses were altogether too beautiful.

Although they each had a king and queen for a father and mother, not one princess was quite to his taste, not one of them was a *real* princess.

One dark night, while a storm crashed and clattered over the kingdom, there was a knock at the castle door. The king himself went down to see who it was.

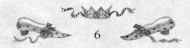

It was a very wet princess. She was so wet that it was difficult to see where her hair stopped and the rain began.

"Who are you?" shouted the king, over the thunderclaps.

"I am a real princess," shouted the wet princess as the lightning ripped the dark clouds apart.

The prince was asleep upstairs, but he woke up when he heard the princess's voice in the hall below.

The queen peered around the door, thinking to herself, "Ah ha! A *real* princess, eh? We'll soon see about that!"

Then out loud the queen said, "Come in! Whoever you are, you can't stay outside in this weather. You shall sleep here tonight."

The wet princess curtsied to the king and queen and came inside, dripping puddles on the hall floor. The prince looked over the stairrail at the princess.

She wasn't too thin,
   she wasn't too fat,
      she seemed to speak his language,
         she had no dogs or horses,
           she didn't wear silly clothes or giggle,
             and she was not too beautiful.

He hoped in his secret heart that she was a real princess.

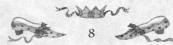

The queen went upstairs to make up the guest bedroom herself.
She took all the bedclothes off the bed and, on the bare wooden slats,
she placed a single pea.

Then she went to the cupboard and brought out twenty mattresses filled
with the softest, downiest feathers in the whole kingdom. On top of the
mattresses she put twenty embroidered silk quilts.

"Come in, my dear," said the queen to the wet princess. "I'll send up some
supper and some dry clothes and you can sleep here tonight."

The wet princess dried herself in front of the great fireplace and put on a
sweetly scented nightdress and ate her supper. She had come a very long way
in the rain and she was very sleepy.

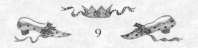

The bed towered above her like a mountain, but she managed to climb up all of the twenty mattresses on nimble toes until she reached the top. Then she cast herself down on the twenty eiderdowns and closed her eyes. In the middle of the night, the queen could not resist peeping into the bedchamber to have a good look at her.

Next morning, when the princess came down to breakfast, the queen asked her, "And how did you sleep, my dear?"

The princess blushed bright red. She knew that it was not polite to be silent when someone asks you a question. But she had also been taught always to speak the truth.

"I'm afraid I couldn't get to sleep at all. I was tossing and turning the whole night through. I think that there must have been something in the bed, for I'm bruised all over."

And the queen looked knowingly at the king, and the king nodded and looked at the prince, and the prince looked at the princess and he smiled.

"You slept on twenty mattresses and twenty quilts and you still felt the pea under them all?" he asked.

The princess nodded.

"Then you must be a *real* princess!" cried the prince.

"It's true, I am," said the Princess, feeling her bruises.

"Only a *real* princess could be so sensitive," said the queen. And the king nodded wisely, and ordered some embrocation for the princess's bruises.

The prince and the princess were married. They put the pea in the royal museum where all the people could see it. And if you don't believe me, you can go and see for yourself!

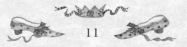

The Mountain Princess

PERSIAN

Once upon a time there was a king whose daughter was named Turandot. She was as beautiful as she was clever. But as she grew up, she studied the art of magic and became less and less human. People said that she was not an ordinary girl at all, but the child of the sun, moon and stars.

Turandot grew even more beautiful, but her heart was like ice. She had the power to make men love her, but she had no love in her heart for any of them. Unfortunately, whoever looked at her, whether prince or peasant, became drunk with love for her. Suitors came from every land to gaze upon her and try to win her hand. When she refused to marry any of them, they would not go away. Soon the palace was filled with heroes and princes sighing with love.

More and more, Turandot would stay in her study and look from the window towards a lofty mountain covered with snow. Like her, it stood alone. Like her, it was cold and single. She called for her father, who could refuse her nothing, and said to him: "Dearest Father, I must go from here. The many suitors who throng our halls are like bees around a hive. Build

for me a strong castle on that mountain so that I can have some peace."

The king was sorry that his daughter wanted to live far away from him, but he granted her request. A great castle with many towers was built for her, its turrets piercing the very clouds themselves. And so Turandot moved into her stronghold with only her servants for company. People called her "the Mountain Princess."

Turandot was happy in her solitude. She could track the stars across the night sky and discover strange inventions and paint her

pictures. To make sure that none of her suitors followed her to the fortress, she made soldiers out of iron and stone to be her watchmen. Whoever came up the mountain path would be killed by the magic swords which the watchmen held in their hands. Turandot also made an invisible gate.

Satisfied that no one would come upon her unawares, Turandot took up her brushes and painted her own life-sized portrait upon fine silk. It was almost more beautiful than the princess because it was painted with a magic brush, and in

the corner she wrote:

> *Prince or hero, to marry me,*
> *These four things must you achieve:*
> *Noble and beautiful you must be;*
> *Through magic swords your way must cleave.*
> *Next you must find the hidden gate;*
> *Answer my riddles or face your fate.*
> *Whoever fails will lose his life,*
> *And never take me as his wife.*

Turandot ordered that this portrait be displayed in the main square of the town. Suitors came from all sides to gaze upon it. Some, suddenly maddened by love of the unattainable princess, set out immediately and were swiftly killed by the magic swords. The heads of those who died were set up over the city gate as a warning to the unwary.

A prince who had not heard about Turandot rode into the town one day and was struck by the radiant face of the fairy princess on the image in the square. The prince felt the incurable pangs of love seize his heart, even as he shuddered with horror when he heard about the terrible fate of her former suitors.

Concealing his passion, he began to think how he might win the princess. Before going to the mountain, he withdrew for a while to the wilderness. There, he discovered a wise hermit living in a cave. He decided to ask the hermit for his advice.

The hermit gazed into dark-blue depths of the night sky. He prayed and watched the stars. Finally, he said to the prince, "I can help you, but you must go to the princess with a pure heart within you."

The prince said, "I do not seek her for my own sake, but for the sakes of all who come to her mountain and find death. I vow to conquer the danger, or may my head also be impaled upon the gate."

The hermit blessed him, and gave him careful instructions, saying, "In token of your vow, put on these blood-red clothes and go forth to the princess's castle without fear."

The prince came to the mountain path where the iron and stone watchmen stood with their sharp swords. As the hermit had told him, the prince dug a trench in the ground and called upon the spirits of the earth. The spirits guided his steps so that none of the magic swords hurt him.

Now the prince reached the top of the mountain. The walls of the fortress rose on every side. As the hermit had told him, the prince took out a drum and struck it. Then he listened carefully to the echoes and soon found the invisible gate.

Turandot had been watching his progress in her magic mirror, which showed her whatever she wanted to see. As soon as he entered the fortress, she sent a message to the prince, "You have been fortunate, adventurer! You have passed through the magic swords unharmed and you have found the invisible gate. Go now to my father's palace and meet me there in two days. Be prepared to answer the riddles I will set."

The prince returned to the town where the people greeted him with joy. He went to the square, took down the portrait of Turandot and gave it to his servant for safekeeping. Next, he took down the skulls of the unhappy suitors and buried them outside the city walls.

On the icy mountain, Turandot, who saw everything in her magic mirror, smiled. She began to wish that this prince might have the key to her mysterious riddles.

Everyone came to the palace to see the princess set the prince her riddles. The king sat on his throne, while Turandot stood behind a curtain where she could see but not be seen.

The king began, "Let the first riddle be set!"

Turandot took one of her earrings and broke off two matching pearls, saying to her servant, "Give these to the prince!"

The prince looked at the pearls and asked for a pair of scales. He weighed them, added three more pearls from his own purse and returned all five to the princess.

The people leaned forward to see what was going on.

Turandot weighed the pearls, crushed them into dust with some sugar, and gave the mixture to the prince. He immediately asked for a glass of milk, then he stirred the pearl-dust into it and sent it back to the princess, who drank it.

The people frowned and muttered. What did this mean?

Then the princess took a brilliant diamond ring from her finger and gave it to the prince. He immediately put it on his own hand and sent her back a beautiful pearl.

Turandot looked at the pearl. She found another of the same size and color on her necklace; she tied them together with thread and gave them to the prince.

The people were baffled. Their muttering grew louder and louder. What kind of riddle could this be?

The prince couldn't see which one was which, so he tied them both to a blue glass marble from his pocket, and sent it back to the princess.

When Turandot saw the marble, she kissed it and tied it onto her wrist. She came out from behind the curtain and said to the king, "Father, please arrange our wedding right away! I have found a husband who is my equal in wisdom!"

The people began to shout and cry out in confusion.

The king looked bewildered, "But, my angel, I don't understand! What went on between you?"

Turandot smiled, "When I sent the prince the two pearls I was saying to him, 'Your life is worth only two days. Make good use of them!' By adding three more pearls, he said to me, 'Even if my life lasted five days, it would pass quickly.'"

"When I first mixed pearl-dust and sugar together, I was saying to him, 'How can I tell true love from false love?' By sending it back to me in a glass of milk, he was saying to me, 'One act of courage separates the true from the false.' And so I drank to his brave deeds that come from a true heart."

"I sent him a ring to show that I consented to marry him. He sent me one great pearl meaning, 'Just as you will never find a second ring like this, so you will never find me a wife who is my equal.'"

Turandot smiled and said, "But I found a great pearl like his in my necklace and sent it to him meaning, 'I am that wife!' And then he had to admit that no two people in the whole world were better suited, so he sent me the blue glass marble to say, 'We are equal under the blue skies of heaven.'"

The king and the people sighed with content. The courage of the prince had melted the icy heart of Turandot so that she was their dear princess again. Turandot was married to the brave prince, who, forever afterwards wore red clothes in memory of that day. The people called him King Redcloak, and he and Turandot reigned in perfect gentleness all the days of their lives.

The Princess who Lost her Hair

AKAMBA (AFRICAN)

Long ago there lived a king who had one daughter. She had a face as clear as glass and eyes like jewels. But from far and wide people came to see her glorious hair which shone like gold.

One day when the princess was in her room, an ugly green bird flew in and spoke to her: "Beautiful princess, I heard everyone say how magnificent you are and now I believe them!"

The princess felt a warm glow in her stomach, for she had never been praised by a speaking bird before. Her father had taught her to be polite to everyone, so she replied, modestly, "Thank you. I know that I am very fortunate and it is wonderful that I have the loveliest hair in my father's kingdom!"

The bird nodded its head, "Indeed it is! Now, as you have so much of it, I wonder if you could spare me some? I need something fine and soft with which to line my nest before I lay my eggs. Please give me a few strands!"

The princess clutched her head and cried in dismay, "Give you my beautiful hair to make a nest? Not one hair will I give you! Fly away quickly, you ugly old bird, before my father's archers shoot you!"

The green bird put its head on one side. "They could not harm me. Now, think again, princess! Will you give me some of your hair?"

"No! No! No! I won't!" she cried.

The green bird flew out of the window and round the tree in the garden, singing:

> *As leaves drop in the dry season's fall;*
> *May this girl have no hair at all.*
> *Leaves return with springtime's rain;*
> *But when will her hair grow again?*

At first the princess was truly frightened by this song, but later she forgot all about it as the year turned.

Then the dry season came. As the leaves fell from the branches, so the princess's hair also began to fall out. Ashamed and angry, the princess hid from everybody until her father came and saw for himself why she was hiding. He listened to her story. Then he called all of the wise women and magicians to him saying, "Whoever brings my daughter's hair back, I will give that person their weight in gold." But no one could do it.

When she awoke, the princess could think of nothing but the dream. She went and told her father what she had dreamt.

Her father called the wise women and magicians together again and bade them look for the seeds of the hair-tree. He promised, "Whoever finds the seeds of that tree, will have his height in gold." But no one had ever heard of such a tree.

In that country there was a poor young man called Muoma. He heard about the princess with no hair. "I will set out myself to find this tree," he said. He traveled to every part of the land, asking the birds, the beasts and the trees if they had heard of the hair-tree.

All the princess's hair fell out, so that she had to remain hidden away in her room. Then one night she had a strange dream. She saw a tree that produced hair and a fine young man who danced round the tree, singing:

Where there is no grass grown,
There shall some seeds be sown,
And golden hair shall be mown.

In her dream the princess also saw the young man plant a seed from which a big tree grew. On its branches grew fruit. As each fruit ripened, so long hair covered it.

But none of them could help him. "I have found nothing upon the land," he thought, "so I will take to the sea."

He sailed in his little boat to a strange island where he found a beautiful golden tree. It stretched up to the sky and at the very top it was shaped like a golden dome. Suddenly the ground shook and the top of the tree exploded, splitting into many pieces. Muoma threw himself to the ground, covering his head. When he arose, he found the ground was covered with red bean pods. He put them into his bag and hurried back to his boat.

As he sailed away, he heard a thunderous sound of great wings. A huge green bird flew down and sat opposite him, asking, "Did you take red beans from the island?"

Muoma nodded fearfully. "Then give me a bean," croaked the bird, "and tell me where you are going."

Muoma told the bird about the princess with no hair.

"Ah, yes! I remember that girl. She refused to give me a few hairs for my nest... Give me another bean and tell me more!"

Muoma fed the bird, trembling, and told it all about the princess's dream.

"That girl should have been more generous! But you will seek long for that tree unless you listen to me!" And the bird told Muoma how to find the hair-tree.

Muoma sailed on and came to a strange place where the trees and flowers walked. There were no people or animals anywhere. As he walked a flower questioned him, "Who are you and what are you looking for?"

"I am a man," said Muoma, "and I am looking for the hair-tree." He told the flower all about his quest to help the princess.

The flower said, "It was good that you gave a bean to the great bird for otherwise it would have eaten you. As you are the first man I have ever met I will help you. But first give me one of the beans, for I too am hungry."

Muoma opened his pouch and fed the flower, who then showed him the way he should follow.

The path became narrow. The wind blew hard. A terrible noise like the crashing of a waterfall filled his ears. It was too hard to remember what the bird and the flower had told him, and Muoma stopped.

In the middle of the path there stood a huge rock. He could go no further. But then he looked again and saw that there was a tiny door in the rock with these words written upon it:

He who knows can pass within:
Fearing nothing, he shall win.

As soon as he read these words, Muoma remembered what he had to say. He whispered these words to the door:

I'm the one who knows, knows,
For the wind blows, blows,
And the water flows, flows;
Here the hair-tree grows, grows,
I'm the one who knows, knows.

The little door sprang open and Muoma was able to enter the rock. Inside was the hair-tree, growing just as in the princess's dream. Quickly, Muoma gathered the hairy fruits and some seeds as well. Then he returned to the king's house.

The king and his daughter were overjoyed to see what Muoma had brought. The wise women and magicians took the long hair from the fruit and put it onto the princess's head. To everyone's surprise, the hair began to grow again, as beautiful as before.

The king thanked Muoma, "My most precious treasure is my daughter and her happiness. As you have restored the joy of all the people, I will give you your weight and height in gold."

From that moment, Muoma was a rich man and the princess a happy woman. She had loved the fine young man who appeared in her dream but now she saw him with her own eyes. The couple lived together in joy for many years, but their children all had black hair like other people.

The Birdcage Husband

KALMUCK (CENTRAL ASIA)

In the land called the Beautiful Flower Garden, there lived a man who owned many herds. His three daughters, who were all princesses, took turns guarding his cattle. One day, while the eldest princess was watching the cattle, she fell asleep and one cow escaped. She quickly followed it and found it going

through a ruby gate,

through a golden gate,

through a gate of mother-of-pearl,

through a gate of emerald,

into a palace of bright treasures where a great white bird sat.

"Have you seen my cow?" asked the princess.

"If you will become my wife, I will give the cow back to you," answered the bird.

The eldest princess put her hands to her cheeks in shame:

All the world would say I was absurd:
Though I lose the cow, I will not wed a bird!

And though she knew her father would beat her for losing one of the herd, she fled from that palace.

The next day, the middle princess went to watch the herd and she also fell asleep. When she awoke she too followed the hoofprints of a stray beast into the enchanted palace. She too met the bird, but, like her elder sister, she would not marry him.

The next day, it was the turn of the youngest daughter. While she was watching the cattle, great sleepiness came upon her, but she jumped up quickly when she saw one of the cows straying. She followed it

through a ruby gate,

through a golden gate,

through a gate of mother-of-pearl,

through a gate of emerald,

into the palace of bright treasures where the great white bird sat.

"Please, white bird, have you seen my cow?" asked the princess.

"If you will become my wife, I will give the cow back to you," answered the bird.

The youngest princess thought quietly. Among her own people everyone kept the promises they made, so she said to the bird:

All the world honors a well-kept word;
Keep your promise and I'll wed you, bird!

The bird and the princess lived together in the palace of bright treasures for many months. The princess saw no one at all except the bird, who sang many tuneful songs to her. But although she enjoyed the songs soon she began to wish for other people to talk to.

One day, a wandering monk came to the palace and told the princess that there was going to be a gathering in honor of the gods. The princess rushed to her husband the bird and said, "Please may I go to the gathering of the tribes? I am lonely and I want to see the world outside this palace..."

The bird bent its long neck. "We will go together! Just carry me there in this cage and put it in a high place where I can see everything. But, be careful who you speak to!" Then the white bird stepped into the cage, the princess latched the door and they set off.

All over the plains people were gathering to make their prayers to the gods. When they had prayed, each one took up a stone and laid it on a pile. Then they made their way to the riding track where the men were competing in races.

"Oh, can I see the horses racing?" begged the princess.

"Certainly," said the white bird. "Set my cage on this post by the horse-enclosure and meet me here at sunset."

The princess rushed off into the throng. Many people turned to look at her as she passed, for she seemed so beautiful and young to be a wife.

Many horsemen raced that day, but the princess only had eyes for the handsome rider of a blue-white horse. He was the best rider there.

A short old woman who stood behind the princess said, "Child, who are the people cheering for? I can't see over the crowd."

"It's the wonderful rider on the blue-white horse," said the princess and she sighed. "If only such a man could be mine! But that can never be, since I have taken a bird as my husband." And she told the old woman her whole story, with tears in her eyes.

The old woman, who was some-thing of a wisewoman, listened to

the princess's story, then said sharply, "Dry your eyes, girl! This rider is your husband: he has been enchanted into the shape of a bird. Listen to me carefully and do as I say, because only you are able to lift the spell that is upon him."

Then the old woman gripped the princess's arm and said, "Pay attention! Go to where you left the birdcage and throw it into a fire. Maybe this will lift the spell from your husband and let him return to his own form."

The princess ran back to the post and found that the cage was indeed empty. She tore it down and thrust it into the fire, happy to think that this would change her husband from a bird into a man again.

As the sun set, the rider on the blue-white horse returned. He saw the princess waiting there and cried out, "Where is my birdcage?"

"I have burnt it," said the princess, smiling.

But the rider did not return her smile: "Unhappy woman! You have burned my soul. Without my soul, I cannot live on earth. I must go far away and serve the gods."

Then the princess began to cry, "Oh, husband, what can I do?"

The rider said, "Go to the palace of bright treasures and stand at the mother-of-pearl gate. You must strike yourself with this horse-stick day and night for seven days. If you stop for an instant, I shall be lost to you forever. If you succeed then I shall be returned to you."

The princess ran all the way back to the palace. She propped her eyelids apart with stalks of grass to keep herself awake. She took up the horse-stick and struck herself for six days and nights, until she was black and blue, but on the seventh day, her eyes began to close.

At that very moment, she heard a wailing cry in the wind and knew that she had lost her husband. She went crying along the dry riverbed calling out, "Oh, Birdcage Husband! Oh, Birdcage Husband!"

For many years, the princess wandered the land looking and calling for him. She thought she heard his voice in the high mountain peaks where the

snow never melts. She thought she heard his voice in the depths of the frozen river.

At last she came to the heap of stones that the people had made on the day that she burned the birdcage. "Mighty gods of the wind and water, bring my birdcage husband to me, I beg you! I don't care whether he is a man or a bird, only bring him back to me."

As she made her prayer, she laid a stone on the heap.

Suddenly, standing in front of her was her husband in the shape of a man. But when she went to touch him, her hands touched only mist for he was a spirit. On his back was a pile of old boots with holes in them. "My heart is joyful to meet you here," he said. "I have been a water-carrier for the gods. I have walked so far that I have worn out all these boots. If you would rescue me from endless journeys, build a birdcage for me and invite my soul back into it."

Out of the long grass, the princess swiftly wove a cage, and sang,

> *Bird or man, take form again!*
> *Soul of my dear, rest you here,*
> *In death or life, I am your wife.*

As soon as she had sung these words, her husband stood beside her as a man and embraced her. "My brave wife, you have rescued me and brought me home to the world of men."

They returned together to the palace of bright treasures and left the birdcage there

> beyond the gate of emerald
> > beyond the gate of mother-of-pearl,
> > > beyond the golden gate,
> > > > so that no one could harm it again.

And together they returned to the tents of the princess's people with the three cows that had strayed. And everyone said that no man or woman were as happy as they.

The Beggar Princess

CHINESE

Once upon a time there lived a young student called Mo Chi. He was a promising student but his prospects were not good. His parents were dead and he had no money.

He thought hard about his problem. Perhaps if he married a rich girl, her family would care for him? He went to the matchmaker who arranged marriages and asked him to find a suitable bride. Although he had no money, he promised the matchmaker a handsome reward, because in those days a bride had to give her money to her husband.

The matchmaker went straight to the court of Chin, the Beggar King. Chin was one of the richest and most powerful men in Hangchow. All the beggars of the city were under his protection. If anyone refused to give money to a beggar, the Beggar King would send round his roughest men to break their windows or sing rude songs outside their house.

The Beggar King had a beautiful daughter called Green Jade. She had been educated like a lady and could read and write, play beautiful music and embroider. But no gentleman would marry her because of her father's position.

The matchmaker sang the praises of Mo Chi to the Beggar King and a marriage was arranged. Chin was delighted that his daughter was to marry a gentleman and move in good society at last. He invited all of Mo Chi's student friends to the wedding.

When Green Jade was unveiled at the ceremony, Mo Chi was pleased by her grace and beauty, which had cost him nothing at all! But as they sat down to the fine feast provided by Chin, a terrible noise broke out. In tumbled all the filthy beggars from the street to sit down with the gentlefolk. They capered about the room, banging their bowls with spoons and pretending to beg from the guests.

Mo Chi shrank back into his seat with horror. He and his friends swiftly rose and left the banquet to the beggars, who swilled it down with relish. Poor Green Jade wept alone in her bed that night.

The next morning, Mo Chi was very polite to his new wife but he was inwardly angry at the humiliation her family had caused him. Green Jade tried to make amends by buying him books, hiring tutors and keeping the house quiet while he studied. Without any thought for herself, she supported him and rejoiced when he passed his final examination. Mo Chi did so well in the examinations that he was chosen to be census officer in the emperor's service.

Now that he could wear a fine black gown and purple sash, he felt angry at being married to the Beggar Princess. He was sure that people everywhere were laughing at him behind his back and saying to each other, "There goes the Beggar King's son-in-law!" So he began to think of ways to get rid of Green Jade.

As he was to take up his new job in a far province, Mo Chi took Green Jade with him. They travelled up the Yellow River by night. "Come, Wife! Come and see the moon," said Mo Chi.

Green Jade rose from her couch and looked in wonder at the high mountains and the huge moon. She had never before been outside the city. "How beautiful the world is," she breathed, entranced by the pale disk of the moon which hung like fruit in the dark and starry sky.

But Mo Chi was thinking other thoughts, "If anyone fell overboard in this darkness, no one would notice. The Yellow River is wide and deep and the body would sink quickly."

He lifted Green Jade in his arms and flung her over the rail into the waters. She screamed in terror and stretched out her arms to him, but her white nightgown became heavy with water and she sank into the flood. The boat swept onwards.

Meanwhile, further downstream, Mo Chi's superior officer, Governor Lord Hsu, was on another riverboat with his wife. As they drank wine and admired the moon, they heard a woman's cry. Their boatman pulled Green Jade out of the waters to safety. Trembling with cold and grief, she told Lord and Lady Hsu her story.

"Do not cry, my dear," said Lady Hsu. "We have no children. Will you consent to be our adopted daughter?"

So Green Jade lived with them at the governor's palace. Lord and Lady Hsu were charmed by her gentleness and good breeding. They suggested that she might take a new husband. With tears in her eyes, Green Jade said, "I may be the Beggar Princess but I have my code of honor. Mo Chi is my husband. I am promised to him and I love him still."

Lord Hsu did his best to help matters. He made it known about the palace that he was looking for a bridegroom for his only daughter: one who would live in their house and be kind to her.

Now, when Mo Chi had arrived at his post, he pretended to be a rich widower. He was able to live like a lord on the money that Green Jade had brought with her when she married him. Now, as a suitor, he sent rich presents to the Hsu household. Lord Hsu felt that Green Jade deserved a better man than Mo Chi, so though he agreed to the wedding, he determined to teach his son-in-law a lesson he wouldn't forget.

The wedding day dawned. Mo Chi dressed in his finest red robes and mounted upon his white steed. "This is the life!" he said to himself, on the road to the palace, "To be a governor's son-in-law is better than being a Beggar King's!"

The women came out to greet him with the wedding song:

> *Golden bridle, horse so fine,*
> *Saddle girt with stitch and sign;*
> *From what quarter comes this lord,*
> *With his fan and silver sword?*

The followers of Mo Chi sang back:

> *A gentleman of city life,*
> *Who has come to claim a wife;*
> *Graduate of studies wise,*
> *Governorship in his fate lies.*

This song wasn't quite true, but Mo Chi meant to be governor himself someday. He dismounted and went into the courtyard for the ceremony. There stood the bride in her red jade slippers and her red veil. Together they bowed to heaven and earth, to Lord and Lady Hsu and to the altar of the ancestors, telling the spirits of the family of their wedding.

Mo Chi's pride was complete. He swaggered into the bridal chamber, at last the husband of a real lady.

Suddenly from behind the screens, out leapt all the women of the household: the aunts and nurses, the maids and slave-girls. They fell upon him, beating him harshly with bamboo rods.

"Save me!" cried out Mo, but the women only scorned and laughed at him. They beat him till his fine robes were in tatters like a beggar's. Snivelling and grovelling on the floor, Mo Chi lay in a miserable heap.

"Stop your beating!" said a sweet voice that he knew.

Mo Chi looked up and beheld his unveiled bride: the face of Green Jade!

"It's a ghost!" he shrieked.

Lord Hsu stepped out from behind the screen, and said sternly, "Oh no! She is no ghost, but our dear adopted daughter whom we saved from the waters of the Yellow River."

Mo Chi knew that he had been found out. He fell upon his knees, "Mercy upon me! I confess my crime. Forgive me!"

Lord Hsu was silent. He looked to Green Jade, encouraging her to speak.

Green Jade's heart was full of pity for her husband, but she spoke hard words to him. "My heart isn't a mat that you can roll up and put away when it suits you," she cried. "When you were poor and unsuccessful, you made use of me. When you grew successful you thought me too low for you. It is true I am lowborn, but I wonder how I could lower myself to wed so despicable a wretch as you?"

Mo Chi clutched her knees, and begged for forgiveness.

Lord Hsu said, "Strangely, I think my daughter still loves you. But perhaps you find our position in society too humble for your ambitions?"

Mo Chi blushed red with shame, "My lord, I am content if Green Jade will accept me as her husband again."

Green Jade raised her husband and kissed him. "We will start again as equals. For I am the governor's daughter, and you are the governor's valued official."

Together the lovers lived with Lord and Lady Hsu. Eventually, Mo Chi became Lord Mo and rose to be governor himself. And when Green Jade's father grew old and sick, it was Lord Mo's pleasure to welcome Chin into their household as a venerable father-in-law.

"When I remember all that the Beggar Princess has done for me, how can I do less for her dear father," he said, bowing before Green Jade. "You have taught me the meaning of nobility, and I will continue to be your student as long as I live."

The Horned Snake's Wife

IROQUOIS

There was once a chief's daughter who could never be content with simple things. Her parents thought that she would never marry because she could not find a man who was unusual enough.

When suitors came to her parents' lodge, she would sit very still and silent, watching each young man. When they had gone, her mother would ask, "Well, daughter, what did you think of him?"

"Oh, he eats too much and belches rudely," she would say. Or, "That one has muddy moccasins." Or, "Did you ever hear such a squeaky voice?"

And it was the same with every man who came to ask to marry her. No matter who came to visit the family lodge, the princess found some fault or other in him.

One night as the fire flickered low, a young man came and scratched at the door.

"Come in, stranger!" said the mother.

But the young warrior lingered in the half-light and stretched out his hand to the chief's daughter. "I have come to take you for my wife," he said, in a

melodious voice that pulled at the girl's heart. He was the most handsome warrior she had ever seen. About his waist was a belt of black and yellow shellbeads that gleamed like water. On his head were two tall feathers that waved like willow wands.

The mother frowned and whispered to her daughter, "You have refused all our braves. Now, will you leave us to marry a stranger whose family we know nothing about?"

The girl nodded. She packed her belongings and followed the handsome warrior. But as she walked beside him through the night, she thought, "Why have I left my mother's lodge? Why am I gone away from my family with a stranger?"

After they had walked for a while, she said out loud, "How near we are to the river! Surely no one lives here?"

Her husband clutched her arm. "Do not fear! Just follow me, we are nearly home among my people."

The girl opened it. Inside was a lovely dress, covered with black and yellow shellbeads that gleamed like water. "Put this on before you meet my people," said her husband.

The dress fascinated and frightened the girl. She leaned over it about to touch it, then pulled away, saying, "I won't put it on! It smells like rotting fish!"

The warrior was angry. "I must go away for a time. Stay here and don't be afraid of anything you see." And his voice, which had been deep and melodious the night before, seemed cold and empty of care for her now.

They climbed down a steep bank. Ahead was a lodge with two horns fastened above the door, like elk-horns. "Come in and be easy," said the smooth voice of her husband. "You will meet my people tomorrow."

All that night, the chief's daughter lay in a half-sleep. There were strange sounds around the lodge, and inside it smelled bad, like rotting fish.

The next day dawned grey and misty. Her husband brought her a parcel of birch bark, "Here is a wedding gift for my new wife," he said with a smile.

After he had gone, the chief's daughter sat alone and thought. She remembered the simple things of home: the fire, her mother sewing quills onto her robe, her father making spears in the sun. She thought of the ordinary men who had asked to marry her and she wept. She was lonely and there was no comfort here.

Just then, a great horned snake crawled into the lodge. The girl sat as still as a stone as the snake peered unblinking into her eyes. As it turned and crawled out of the door, she saw that its body glittered black and yellow in the misty light.

She peered outside. All over the rocks and by the river bank there were horned snakes, coiled and crawling about. It was then that she realized the truth. Her fine husband was really a snake disguised in human form!

Now though she had been foolish, the chief's daughter was not without courage and wisdom. She knew very well that she had done the right thing by refusing to put on the dress. If she had put it on, she would have become a snake herself. But what could she do?

Frightened though she was, that night she fell into a deep sleep. And as she slept, she dreamed. An old man came to her and said in a kind, clear voice,

52

"Granddaughter, you are distressed. Do you want me to help you?"

"Oh, Grandfather, please do! I know that I have acted foolishly. What can be done now?"

"Do as I say," said the old man. "Leave this place quickly and run to the edge of the village. There you will find a steep cliff. Climb up it and never turn back or your husband's people will get you. When you reach the clifftop I will help you again."

As the girl awoke, she saw her husband coming into the lodge, dressed in his beautiful human shape. His arms were outstretched to embrace her. Quick as a partridge, she dashed under his arms, out of the lodge and ran away as fast as the wind.

Behind her, her husband's smooth voice called, "Come back!" but she didn't look back.

As she climbed, she felt a rustle, like the autumn breeze whispering through the trees and her husband's voice came to her again, like the hissing of a snake, "Come back, wife, and join my people."

Hand over hand, she pulled herself up the steep rocks. "Grandfather, help me now! I can go no further!" she called into the sky.

Just as her feet began to stumble, she felt a mighty hand lifting her up. The figure of the old man was now revealed to her: he was none other than Heno the Thunderer, a mighty spirit of her people. The chief's daughter hid her face in her hands.

Heno began to throw his thunderspears down upon the horned snakes. The lightning split open the sky and the drumming of thunder throbbed in the air. Wherever the horned snakes tried to crawl, the thunderspears of Heno struck them down.

When all the snakes lay still, the chief's daughter lifted her face to the gentle rain. It washed away the tears from her face and the smell of the horned snakes from her body.

Heno the Thunderer looked down at her, "Bravely done, my young granddaughter! You have helped me rid the earth of these monsters and your action has given you special power. It may be that I shall call on you again, for there is a bond between us now."

Heno summoned a cloud and placed the chief's daughter upon it. The cloud carried her gently down to her own village, where her parents and people greeted her with great joy.

Soon enough, the chief's daughter married an ordinary man. He had a good heart: he sang cheerily in the mornings, hunted well at midday and snored at nights. But he never glittered black and yellow as water, or smelled of rotten fish. Together, they had many fine children. Sometimes, Heno the Thunderer would call upon the chief's daughter to fly with him and help rid the earth of bad-hearted creatures. Among her people, the chief's daughter was a wise woman.

But when she was old she always gave the same advice to her grandchildren, "The world is wide and there are many strange things in it. Best be content with simple things!"

The Sleeping Beauty

GERMAN

Long ago, there lived a king and queen who were sad because they had no children. One day the queen was sitting and weeping in her bath when a frog hopped out of the water and said, "Dear Queen, don't cry so! Before a year is over, a daughter will be born to you."

The frog's words came true. The queen gave birth to a beautiful baby girl. The king was so happy that he gave a grand party. He invited his family and friends and the most important people in his kingdom — the fairies who had the power to grant wishes. He wanted his baby daughter to receive their special blessing.

Now, there were thirteen fairies in that country, but because the king had only twelve golden plates for his very important guests, he sent out only twelve invitations.

When the party was at its most merry, the herald blew his trumpet and called out, "Silence for the most excellent fairies." One by one, the fairies came forward to lean over the princess's magnificent cradle and breathe their blessings upon the baby.

The first fairy said, "Beauty."

The second said, "Riches."

The third said, "Joy."

The fourth said, "Wisdom."

The fifth said, "Love."

The sixth said, "Pleasure."

The seventh said, "Innocence."

The eighth said, "Truth."

The ninth said, "Delight."

The tenth said, "Trust."

The eleventh said, "Gentleness."

The twelfth fairy was about to speak, when suddenly the doors of the palace flew open. A great wind filled the hall and blew out the candles, so that the only light came from the twelve tips of the fairies' wands.

In through the doors strode the thirteenth fairy who had not been invited. She was purple with rage at having been forgotten. Without greeting a soul, she leaned over the baby's cradle, and in a ghastly voice said, "When she is fifteen-years-old, the princess will prick her finger on a spindle and fall down dead!" Then she swept out of the hall again.

The king and queen wrung their hands in anguish. But the twelfth fairy came forward and said, "Fear not! I have still to grant my blessing. The princess will not die! Instead she will fall into a deep sleep that will last for a hundred years."

This last blessing cheered the royal couple and gave them hope, but just to make sure no harm could come to the princess, the king ordered that all spindles in the land should be destroyed.

The princess grew up to be all the things that the fairies had wished upon her: she was fortunate, lovely, sweet-natured and kind, and everyone loved her. Her parents gave her everything that a girl could desire, but whenever she left the castle, many servants accompanied her, to make sure that she never found a spindle.

The princess grew tired of always being with her servants. She longed to be alone, and to have an adventure. So after promising on no account to leave the castle she dismissed her servants and went exploring.

She explored the castle dungeons, which were dark and empty except for a mouse.

She peered down the well in the kitchen courtyard and saw her own reflection.

She went and sat on her father's throne in the throne room and tried on her mother's crown.

She discovered a funny map in the library. She tried on some old-fashioned clothes that she found in a cupboard.

She threw cherrystones down from the balcony onto the soldiers' helmets, and when they shouted at her, she ran laughing up a long narrow staircase in a lonely tower.

In the door at the top of the winding stair was a rusty key. She turned the key with both hands and the door fell open with a creak. Inside sat an old woman spinning flax into thread.

"Good day to you, old woman," said the princess. "What is it that you are doing?"

"I'm spinning," she replied.

The princess stared at the spindle in the old woman's hands that danced and spun so merrily. She had never seen anything like it.

"What is that thing in your hands that hums and spins?" she asked.

"This is my merry dancer who makes flax into thread," said the old woman, gravely.

"Oh, do let me try!" begged the princess, her fingers itching.

And before you could say "four-and-twenty blackbirds," the princess had pricked her finger on the spindle and instantly fell upon the floor in a deep sleep.

And as the magic worked, so the spindle flew out of the princess's hand and danced all over the castle. Wherever it spun, everything stopped and everyone fell asleep.

The king and queen slept in their council chamber, the soldiers slept on the battlements and the servants slept in the kitchen. Everyone in the castle fell into a deep sleep.

The flies slept on the walls, the horses in the stables, the pigeons on the roofs, the dogs under the tables, the mouse in the dungeons. Every creature within the gates fell asleep.

The fire in the hearth stopped in mid-flame, the clocks in the halls, the leaves on the trees, even the flag on the topmost tower was still. Everything fell into a deep slumber.

And all around the castle there grew up a great spiky hedge of briars. It grew and grew until the battlements were hidden from sight.

The years passed, and the people from the country round about often spoke of the beautiful sleeping princess in her castle of thorns. The story of Briar Rose spread to every land, and many people tried to find the way through the spiky hedge to see if the story was true. Many brave adventurers tore their hands apart on the thorns and some even died.

Then one day, a hundred years later, a prince heard the story of Briar Rose. His heart burned inside him when he thought of the beautiful princess and all her family and servants asleep within the enchanted hedge. He made up his mind to rescue her.

When the prince saw what a dark thicket of briars surrounded the castle, his courage nearly failed him. But as he drew closer, the hedge began to burst into flower. Great pink, gold and white roses opened, and the spiny thorns withdrew as he approached. He was able to walk through the hedge without harm, but it closed up behind him as he went in the castle gates.

Then he made his way through the castle. He saw with wonder that, although a hundred years had passed, there was no dust anywhere. There was no sign of age upon the sleeping forms who stood or lay where they had fallen so long ago.

The prince saw the fire that still flamed but did not give heat, the cook still stirring the pot, the soldiers slumped at their posts and the mouse just about to eat the cheese. Nothing breathed or moved, not even the clock. The only thing that hung in the air was the scent of roses.

He found the narrow, winding staircase. The scent of roses was even stronger here. He entered the little tower-room where the princess lay, lovely and still as one who is dead. Her skin, lips and hair were the color of rose-petals — white and pink and golden.

He touched his lips very gently to hers. Very slowly, her breathing rose and fell like one who is asleep. And very, very slowly, she opened her eyes and looked with delight upon the prince.

And as the princess woke up, so all the castle awoke.

The pigeons took flight from the battlements, the leaves began to dance and quiver, the horses whinnied and kicked in their stables.

The fire flickered into life, the servants began to bustle about their work, the king and queen raised their heads from the table in the council chamber and the flag on the tower fluttered once more in the wind.

The hedge of briars shrank magically back into the earth and everything was as it had been before.

The prince and Briar Rose were married and lived very happily. And the king gave them a set of thirteen golden dishes for a wedding present.

Sources for the Stories

The Princess and the Pea

This tale is based on Hans Christian Andersen's retelling of a folk story that is found all around the world. Sometimes the test of a real princess is to be put into a bed with something uncomfortably sharp, like a stone or a knitting needle. By contrast, in some Persian and Indian versions of this theme, the flesh of noble princesses is so sensitive that it is burned or bruised by the fall of leaves or lotus flowers.

The Horned Snake's Wife

I learned this Iroquois story during a visit to storytelling friends in Vermont. Its theme – the girl who marries a man with both a human and animal shape – is common to all countries in the world. Stories of alliances between a snake and a girl are common in the creation myths of North America.

The Princess Who Lost Her Hair

Can anything be worse for a girl than having no hair? This story appealed to me when I heard it told at an Afro-Caribbean story festival in North Kensington, London, in 1984. The lesson of grudging generosity being paid back by removal of what we fail to share is one that animals often teach human beings in folk tales.

The Birdcage Husband

This story was collected by the indefatigable traveler and folklorist C. Fillingham Coxwell, who heard it on his sojourn among the nomadic Kalmuck people of the region that borders Siberia and Mongolia. He recorded the story in *Siberian and other Folk Tales* (1925). The soul appears in bird form in many cultures. Here, the birdcage is the soul's home.

The Beggar Princess

All over the world, the status of girls is often considerably lower than that of boys. In this wise Chinese story, the daughter of the King of Beggars is considered to be expendable by her husband, but he is brought to appreciate her again. This story, that I heard at a storytelling festival in London a few years ago, is one that I like to tell to girls who say "but it isn't fair," when they come off worse against boys.

The Mountain Princess

The story comes from the work of the 12th century Persian poet Nizami, one from a series of delightful stories about seven princesses who live in seven different colored pavilions that correspond to the planets. The Turandot story is told by the princess in the red pavilion of Mars. The complex riddles and hidden meanings of the lovers in this story are common to Persian love stories.

The Sleeping Beauty

This is the Grimm Brothers' variant of a folk tale known all over Europe. Perrault's *La Belle au Bois Dormant* is another well-loved version.

Barefoot Books 2067 Massachusetts Ave, Cambridge, MA 02140. Text copyright © 1997 by Caitlín Matthews. Illustrations copyright © 1997 by Olwyn Whelan. The moral right of Caitlín Matthews to be identified as the author and Olwyn Whelan to be identified as the illustrator of this work has been asserted. First published in the United States of America in hardcover in 1998 by Barefoot Books Inc. This paperback edition first printed in 2000. All rights reserved. No part of this book may be reproduced in any form or by any means, electronic or mechanical, including photocopying, recording or by any information storage and retrieval system, without permission in writing from the publisher. Graphic design by Judy Linard, London. Printed and bound in China by Printplus Ltd. Printed on 100% acid-free paper. Paperback ISBN 978-1-84148-172-2
Library of Congress Cataloging in Publication Data is available upon request.
11 13 15 14 12